King Midas and the

A Greek My[...]

retold by Laura Layton Strom

illustrated by Kirk Parrish

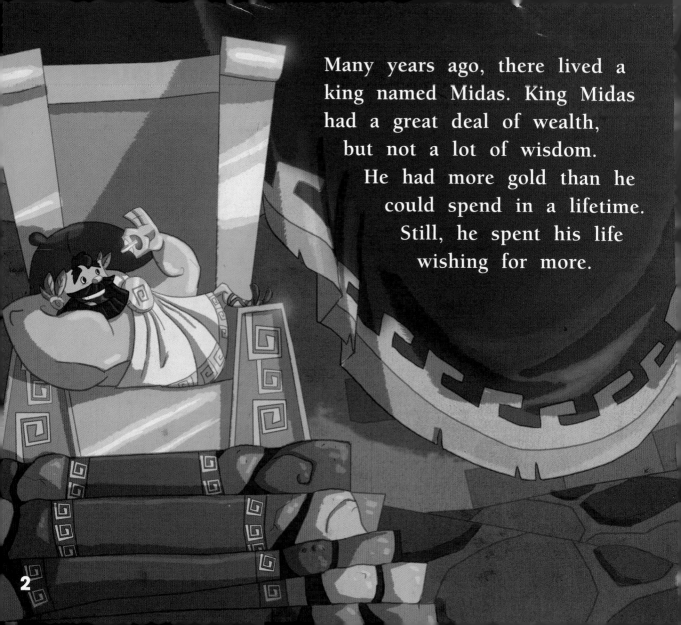

Many years ago, there lived a
king named Midas. King Midas
had a great deal of wealth,
but not a lot of wisdom.
He had more gold than he
could spend in a lifetime.
Still, he spent his life
wishing for more.

The king had one little daughter, whose name was Marigold. His daughter was his pride and joy. She was as sweet as honey and as gentle as a kitten. There was only one thing he loved more than his daughter—gold!

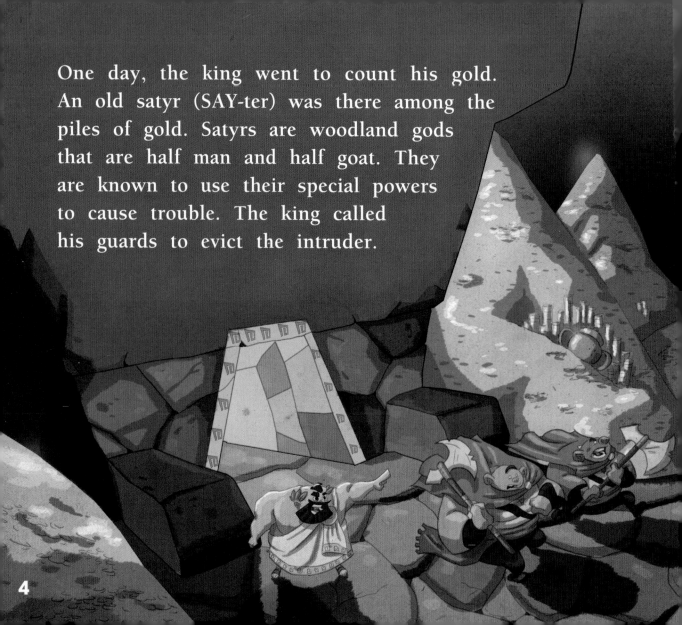

One day, the king went to count his gold.
An old satyr (SAY-ter) was there among the
piles of gold. Satyrs are woodland gods
that are half man and half goat. They
are known to use their special powers
to cause trouble. The king called
his guards to evict the intruder.

"Wait," sang the goat-like man.
"I hear you are the richest
in the land.
"No other has such gold
in his command."

This got King Midas's attention.

"That is quite true, quite true," he responded.
"As you can see, I have this room full of
gold, but I wouldn't mind having even more.
Gold is the best and most wonderful thing
in the whole world! I love gold!"

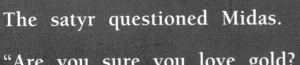

The satyr questioned Midas.

"Are you sure you love gold?
"That statement is quite bold!"

"I am quite sure," answered the king confidently. Then he remembered that the satyr was not invited.

"Guards! Take away this intruder!" called King Midas.
The guards came running with their axes raised.

The sly satyr spoke up quickly.

"Well this is quite a kettle of fish.
But I can grant you one little wish," he sang.

A wish? thought the king, smiling broadly.
"Tell me more!" he demanded.

The satyr asked King Midas,
"If I could grant one wish to behold,
would you ask for even more gold?"

The king's mouth watered. He rubbed his hands together greedily at the thought.

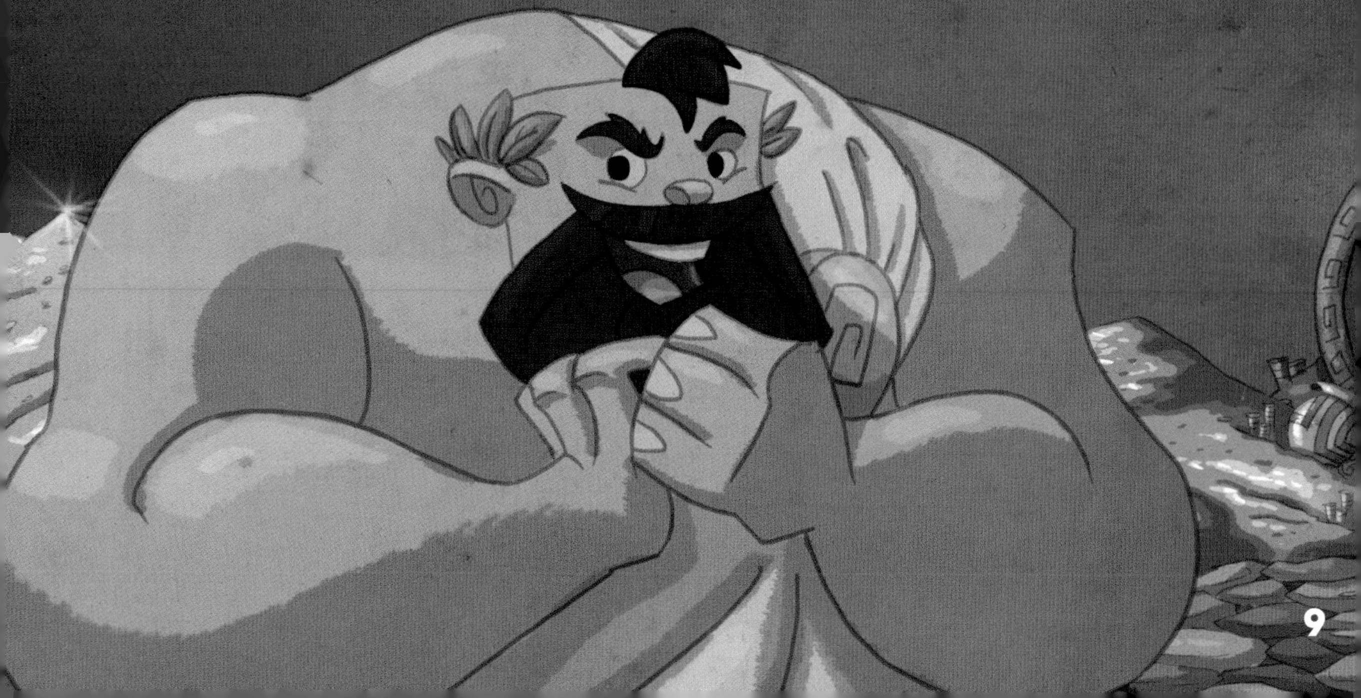

"If I could have but one wish," said the king,
"I would ask that everything I touch be turned
to BEAUTIFUL, SHINY GOLD!"

The satyr chanted,
"Your wish is my command!
So as sunrise kisses the land,
Your slightest touch, all within your clutch,
will turn to gold. It has been foretold!"

He paused. "I must add," he chimed.
"This gift will not make you glad."

"Nonsense," said the king.
"Gold is my greatest joy.
I will take the risk."
He turned to his guards.
"Let him be." And with
that the satyr disappeared.

The next day, King Midas awoke very early. He was eager to see if the satyr's promise had come true. As soon as the sun rose, he touched his pillow with his hand. It instantly turned to gold! He stood up and touched a chair and table. They both turned to solid gold!

"I will be the richest king in the world!" cried Midas.

All the excitement made King Midas hungry.
He went into his banquet hall and called for a feast.
He smiled when he sat on his royal bench, and it
turned to gold. His smile brightened when he touched
his table and it turned to gold.

But when he picked up a tasty loaf of bread,
and it turned to gold, his smile faded. When
he picked up a glass of cold water,
the water became solid gold, too.
He couldn't eat or drink a thing!
All was GOLD, GOLD, GOLD.
Midas grew hungrier and thirstier.

"What a fool I have been!" Midas moaned, too lost in his misery to see that his daughter had entered the hall. Marigold had never seen her father so sad. She rushed to him and gave him a hug.

"Don't!" Midas cried, but it was too late. The hug turned Marigold into a golden statue.

All of the joy disappeared from the king's life.

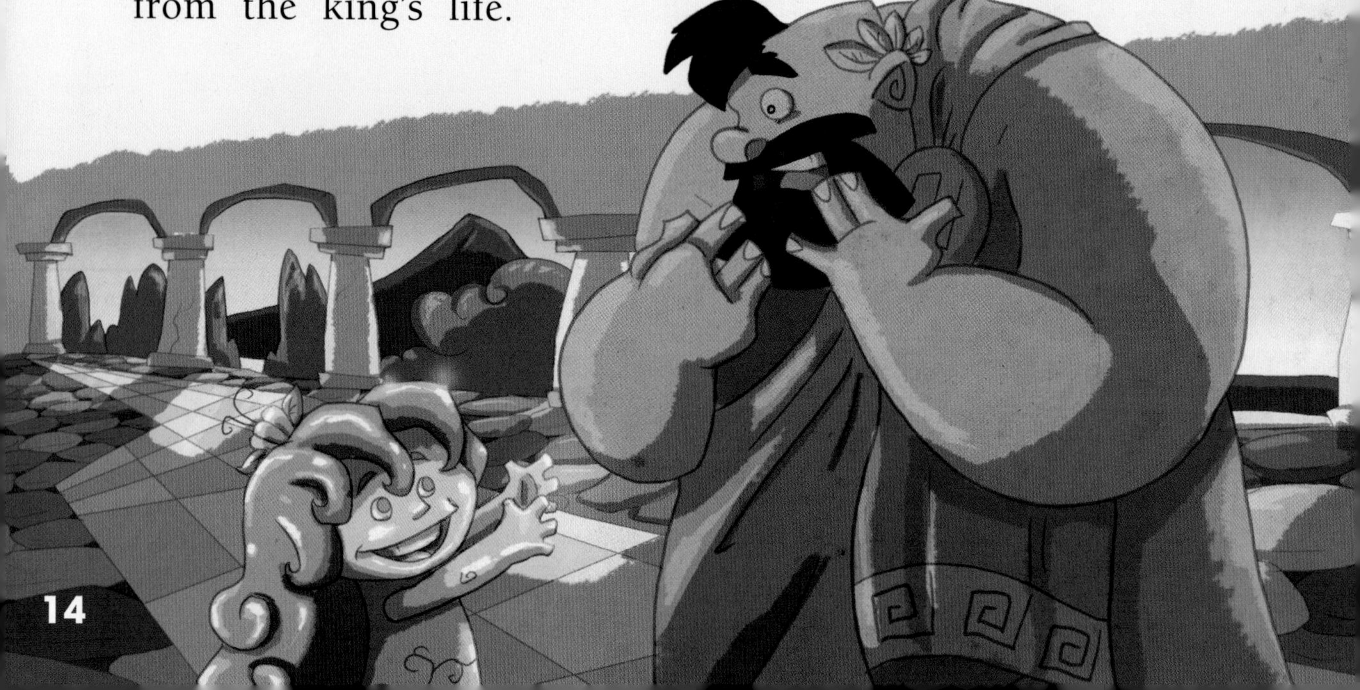

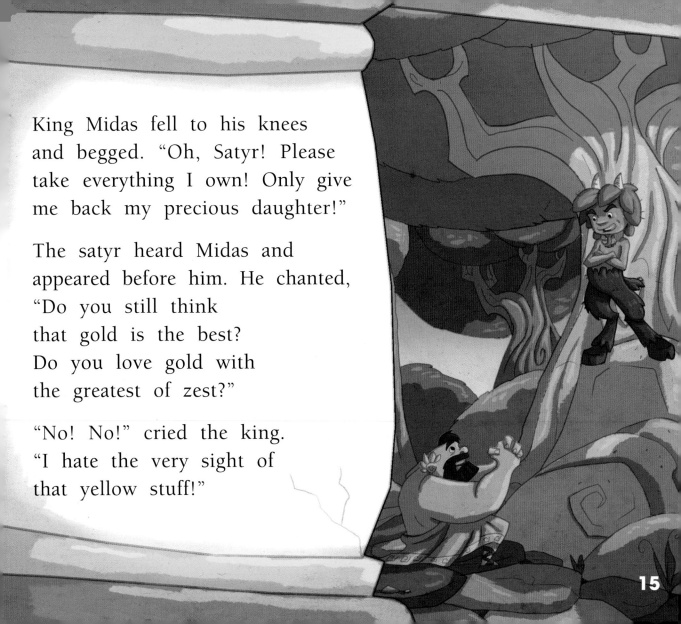

King Midas fell to his knees
and begged. "Oh, Satyr! Please
take everything I own! Only give
me back my precious daughter!"

The satyr heard Midas and
appeared before him. He chanted,
"Do you still think
that gold is the best?
Do you love gold with
the greatest of zest?"

"No! No!" cried the king.
"I hate the very sight of
that yellow stuff!"

"Then take this pitcher from the spring.
Sprinkle your hands, sprinkle anything.
The drops will dissolve the golden touch,
and you will be with whom you love so much."

And all turned back to what was before—almost all.

King Midas learned that there were riches
greater than gold.